"For children who are st... ...own,
Tony Wilkinson's *Hector* ... is gr... ..."
Harpers & Queen

Tony Wilkinson is a writer, cartoonist and broadcaster.
He worked for BBC radio's *Today* programme then
spent several years as a television reporter on
Nationwide, *Brass Tacks*, *Moment of Truth* and
Watchdog before returning to BBC radio with his own
programmes, *Wilko's Weekly* and *The Street*. His strip
cartoons have appeared in both *The Guardian* and
The Times. His comic-strip book *Scoop and Hudson
and the Deadly Germ* is also published by Walker
Books. Tony Wilkinson is married with two sons and
lives in north London.

TONY WILKINSON

Illustrations by Tony Wilkinson

WALKER BOOKS

AND SUBSIDIARIES

LONDON • BOSTON • SYDNEY

For Rory and Gray

First published 1994 by
Walker Books Ltd, 87 Vauxhall Walk
London SE11 5HJ

This edition published 1995

6 8 10 9 7 5

© 1994 Tony Wilkinson

This book has been typeset in Garamond.

The right of Tony Wilkinson to be identified as author of this work
has been asserted by him in accordance with the
Copyright, Designs and Patents Act 1988.

Printed and bound in Great Britain by The Guernsey Press Co. Ltd

British Library Cataloguing in Publication Data
A catalogue record for this book is
available from the British Library.

ISBN 0-7445-3687-1

J109,674 £3.99

CONTENTS

Hector the rat was a disgrace to his family. He was clean. He worked hard. He was kind.

Hector's mother, father, brothers, sisters, cousins, aunts, uncles and grandparents were all ashamed of Hector. They said rats should be dirty, low-down and mean.

They gave him a final warning.
Unless Hector began to behave
badly at once, he would be thrown
out of the family sewer, never to
return.

Hector tried to be dirty, low-down
and mean, but it was hopeless.

When his brothers and sisters
went scavenging in dustbins for
food, Hector tidied up after them.

When his father bit strangers in
the street, Hector apologized to
them and bandaged their wounds.

When his mother ordered him
to dirty his room, Hector cleaned it
from top to bottom.

To make matters worse, Hector began to read books. He found them on the rubbish dump. He read books about spaceships. He read books about pirates, monkeys and maps. He read encyclopedias from cover to cover.

One book taught him how to
juggle. The next day he performed
for the dogs and cats in the alley
at the back of the hamburger bar.
They were amazed. The richer dogs
threw money into his hat.

Hector's family was not impressed.
A meeting was called to discuss his
behaviour.

"If he wants money, he should
steal it!" snarled his brother, Fang.
"How are we supposed to terrorize
the neighbourhood when he goes
around smiling and being nice?"

"He'd rather read a book than pick a fight," sneered his sister Slymella.

"And he's disgustingly clean!" said his grandmother, licking her feet. "Last week I caught him eating off a plate instead of the floor."

"From today," said his father,
"Hector is no longer a member of
our family."

CHAPTER TWO

So Hector was expelled from the
family sewer.

He had never been above-ground
by himself. It was a scary place.

Huge machines with wheels roared past. Fierce winds followed in their path. Hector was almost blown over.

Giants stamped past in heavy shoes. The pavements shook.

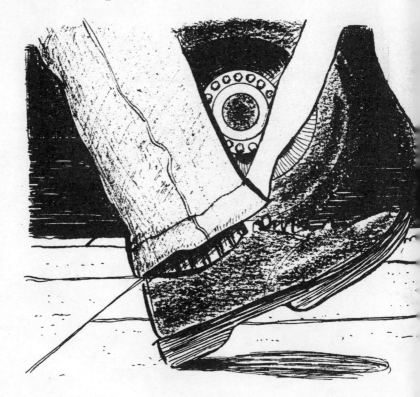

Hector asked several of them if they could help him find a new home, but they did not reply.

"Maybe they can't speak," thought Hector. "Or perhaps they are too high up to hear me."

He wandered the streets for
hours, lost and lonely. By nightfall,
he had arrived at the city park.

He felt tired. He lay down under a bush, and covered himself with a blanket of old newspapers.

It was difficult to sleep. There were frightening noises – rustlings and hootings and scufflings. It was a long time before morning came.

He was woken by the sound of a
bicycle bell. "Go away," said Hector.
"I'm trying to sleep."

"Amazing!" said a boy, peering
under the bush. "A talking rat!"

"Astonishing!" said Hector.
"A talking giant!"

"I'm not a giant, I'm Charlie," said
the boy. "I live round the corner."

"You mean..." said Hector. "You
mean ... you've got a home?"

"Hasn't everyone?" said Charlie.

"I haven't," said Hector.

"Well, you have now," said Charlie. "I always wanted a pet rat."

"A pet?" said Hector. He had never heard the word before.

"It's what my mum won't let me have," said Charlie. "But she's bound to like you."

CHAPTER THREE

So Charlie took Hector home to
number nine Clover Gardens.

"That's where I live," said Charlie.

"Above the ground!" said Hector.

"Whoopee!"

27

Charlie's smile faded when he saw a van parked in the road.

"Quick, hide!" he said. "It's the rat-catcher!"

But it was too late. Running towards them was a huge, evil-looking man with a big cage.

Hector jumped into the luggage box on the back of Charlie's bike.

But the rat-catcher had spotted him and began to shout.

"Hold tight," said Charlie, turning his bike around. "We'll have to make a dash for it."

Charlie pedalled as fast as he could, but the rat-catcher was gaining ground. Charlie swerved round parked cars, hoping to shake him off, but the rat-catcher followed close behind.

Without warning, Charlie's
bicycle squealed to a stop.
Their way was blocked. Workmen
inspecting the sewer had put up
a safety barrier across the road.

"Quick!" shouted Hector.

Charlie scrambled after Hector
down a hole in the road. Inside was
a ladder which led to the sewer far
below.

Within seconds, the rat-catcher followed. But he did not get far. He was too big. Try as he might, he could not squeeze himself down the hole. Soon, he was stuck. The more he wriggled, the worse it became. He used words which could only be found in the rat-catcher's dictionary.

Ratznoig!

Drang!

Sturm!

"We're safe now," said Hector.

Charlie was not so sure.

"It's very dark," he said. "How will we get out?"

"Rateral thinking," said Hector. "We rats are famous for it. Watch."

CHAPTER FOUR

Hector put his hand deep into his
pocket. He pulled out some string,
a tiny rat-sized torch, a magnetic
compass, two boiled sweets,
a toothbrush and a piece of paper
which he unfolded carefully.

"It's a secret map of the sewer,"
he said. "I made it myself."

"What's the sewer?" said Charlie.

"This is," said Hector. "It's a big
tunnel under the street. There are
hundreds of them. The water from

all the houses comes down pipes and ends up in the sewer."

"You mean there's a sewer under every street?" said Charlie.

"Yes," said Hector. "Look at the map. This one goes underneath Cassidy Street, along Plumpton Crescent and into Clover Gardens."

"But that's where I live!" said Charlie, excitedly. "Could we ... you know ... could we walk underground to number nine?"

"As easy as winking," said Hector. "Look, there it is, third sewer on the left, ninth pipe along. We'll be able to climb out of the manhole at the end."

"Tie this string around your waist," said Hector. "Steady yourself with your hands against the walls. I'll lead you."

Charlie touched the smooth bricks of the tunnel. They were cold and wet and slippery.

He felt the string pull tight around his waist and he heard Hector's footsteps ahead.

"How can you see where you're going?" he whispered.

"My eyes are used to the dark," said Hector. "Come on. This way."

After a while Hector stopped to check his compass bearing.

"North, north-west fifty paces, south-west twenty paces. We'll soon be there!"

Suddenly, they heard footsteps.

"Quick!" said Hector. "In here!"

Four mean-looking sewer rats scuttled past.

"My cousins," hissed Hector. "If they find me here, we're done for."

"You mean they'd hurt us?" said Charlie.

"Worse," said Hector. "They'd steal my map. Then we'd never find our way out."

When the coast was clear, they set off again. Hector kept looking behind to make sure no one was following. Five minutes later, he stopped and smiled.

They entered the sewer which ran underneath Clover Gardens. On the right-hand side was a row of numbered holes.

"What was the number of your house?" asked Hector.

"Nine."

They walked another five paces.

Hector put his ear to the hole marked number nine.

"Does your mum ever sing a song called 'Yellow Submarine'?" he said.

"She never stops," said Charlie. "How did you know?"

"She's singing it now. You can hear it down the pipe."

Charlie leaned closer. "You're right! She's cleaning the bathroom…" A look of panic came across his face. "Oh, no! That's my job. I'd better get home quick!"

They listened hard for the sound of cars before lifting the manhole cover at the end of Charlie's street.

"I'll go home and ask my mum if you can stay," said Charlie. "You go back down the ladder and wait."

"Are you sure she'll say yes?"

"Of course!" said Charlie.

CHAPTER FIVE

But Charlie's mother did not
say yes.

"A pet rat?" she cried. "Never!
How many times do I have to tell
you?"

Charlie was upset. He locked himself in the bathroom, sat on the edge of the bath and wept. Tears splashed down. He sobbed and sobbed.

Then, a small voice was heard from somewhere far below. "Hector to Charlie! Can you hear me? Over."

It seemed to be coming from the plug hole of the washbasin. Charlie leaned over to hear more.

"Hector to Charlie. Cheer up! Over."

49

And that's exactly what they did,
though Hector didn't like being in
Charlie's bag. It muddled him up.

"You're in the broom cupboard,"
said Charlie.

"Where?"

"In my house, of course."

Hector poked out his head.
There were piles of junk all around.

"What a mess!" said Hector.
"I could tidy it up if you like."

"Shhh! No noise!" said Charlie.
"My mum's in the kitchen. She'll
hear!"

But no sooner had Charlie closed
the cupboard door than a terrible
banging and clattering began.

Charlie's mother bustled down the hallway, flung open the cupboard door and found … the tidiest cupboard she had ever seen!

She looked amazed. "Did you tidy the cupboard, Charlie?" she said.

Charlie was too busy trying to see where Hector was hidden.

"Well, Mum, I er… you see, I er…"

"Well done, Charlie! Good boy, Charlie!" And she went back to the kitchen, humming "Yellow Submarine".

In the next few days, Charlie got used to being praised by his mother. Whenever her back was turned, Hector would sneak out of his cupboard and tidy something.

First, he tidied Charlie's messy bedroom – after they'd had a wonderful pillow fight.

Then he tidied Charlie's toy drawer – after they had played with every one of the toys. He tidied the living-room, the clothes cupboards, the kitchen, the bathroom – everywhere from the front hallway to the back bedroom.

Twice he was nearly caught. The first time, he had to disguise himself as a milk jug. He curled up his tail so that it looked just like a jug handle and pointed his nose to look like a spout.

The second time, he pretended to be a telephone. He coiled up his tail to look like curly cable. Luckily, no one telephoned.

Charlie's mother was so pleased, she bought Charlie ice-cream and videos. She told all the neighbours how good he had been. It was embarrassing. Charlie was getting praised for everything Hector had done.

CHAPTER SIX

By the end of the week, Charlie could stand it no longer. He sat down and wrote his mother a note.

Dere mum
It wasn't me what tidied up. It was my friend Hector the rat. Can I keep him as a pet?
Pleese, pleese, pleese.
Charlie

Charlie's mother didn't believe him, of course. She thought the idea of a rat who tidied cupboards and toy drawers and kitchens was one of Charlie's best jokes ever.

She pushed a note under Charlie's bedroom door saying that of course he could keep his invisible friend. Only he should make sure that she never saw Hector or she would be very frightened.

"She thinks you're imaginary!" said Charlie. "She believes I'm making you up!"

"But this is wonderful news," said Hector.

"Why?" said Charlie.

"Well, if I don't exist, you don't ever have to ask if you can keep me. I can stay here with you for ever!"

"And be my secret pet?"

"Yes."

And that's just what Hector did.

AUTHOR'S NOTE

You may have noticed that Charlie isn't very good at spelling. Can you help him on page 57?

MORE WALKER SPRINTERS
For You to Enjoy

☐ 0-7445-3667-7   *Taking the Cat's Way Home*
by Jan Mark/Paul Howard   £3.50

☐ 0-7445-3183-7   *The Baked Bean Kids*
by Ann Pilling/Derek Matthews   £3.50

☐ 0-7445-3665-0   *The Biggest Birthday Card in the World*
by Alison Morgan/Carolyn Dinan   £3.99

☐ 0-7445-3091-1   *The Finger-eater*
by Dick King-Smith/Arthur Robins   £3.99

☐ 0-7445-3666-9   *Beware the Killer Coat*
by Susan Gates/Josip Lizatović   £3.50

☐ 0-7445-3664-2   *Gemma and the Beetle People*
by Enid Richemont/Tony Kenyon   £3.99

☐ 0-7445-3668-5   *Impossible Parents*
by Brian Patten/Arthur Robins   £3.99

**Walker Paperbacks are available from most booksellers,
or by post from B.B.C.S., P.O. Box 941, Hull, North Humberside HU1 3YQ**

24 hour telephone credit card line 01482 224626

To order, send: Title, author, ISBN number and price for each book ordered, your full
name and address, cheque or postal order payable to BBCS for the total amount and allow
the following for postage and packing: UK and BFPO: £1.00 for the first book, and 50p
for each additional book to a maximum of £3.50. Overseas and Eire: £2.00 for the first
book, £1.00 for the second and 50p for each additional book.

Prices and availability are subject to change without notice.

Name _____

Address _____

_____